I0713616

For prize giveaways, free content, book giveaways, and more please e-mail us and tell us you want to be included on our e-mail list.

Visit us online at

www.touchtheskypublishing.com

Please take the time to leave us a good review.

Touch the Sky
Publishing

www.ingramcontent.com/pod-product-compliance
Lightning Source LLC
Chambersburg PA
CBHW080909190726
48294CB00008B/2026